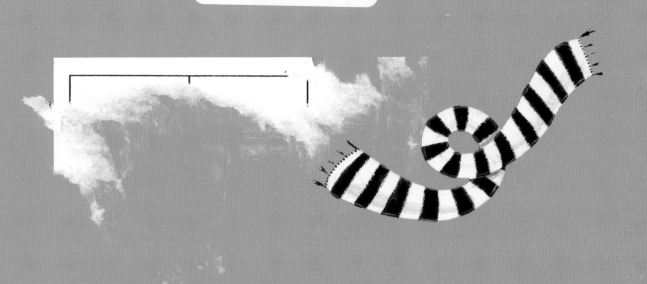

Zippity Zebra

and the Windy Day

Claire Henley

SCHOLASTIC

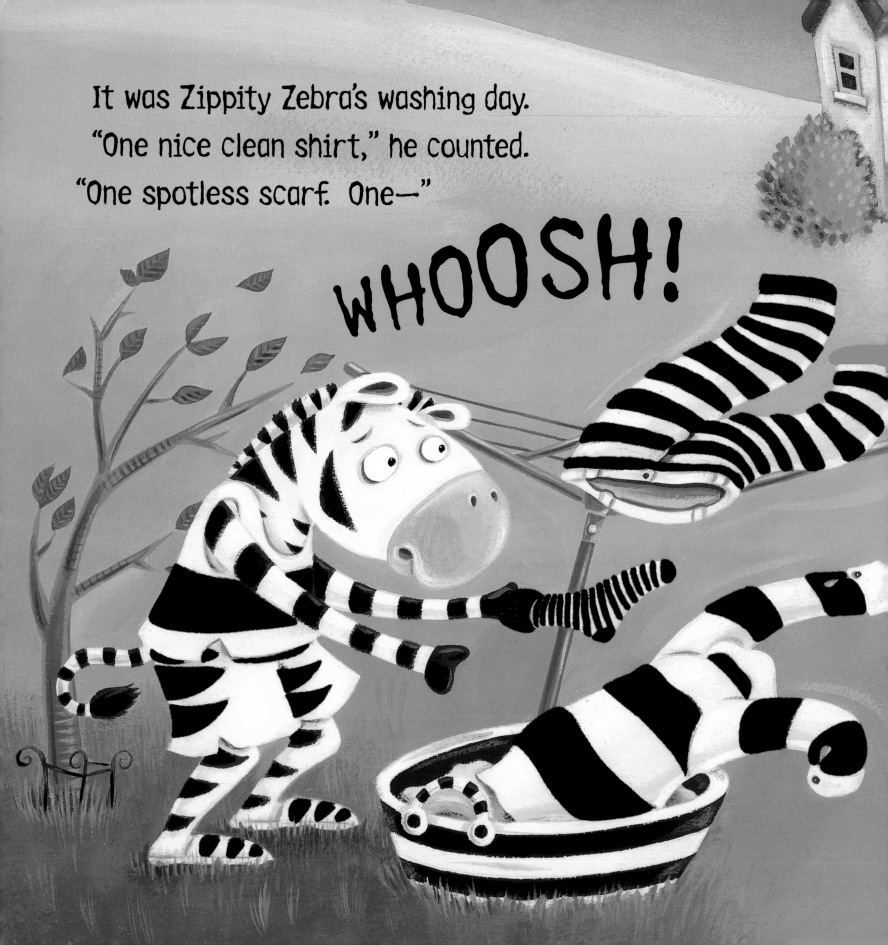

It was Zippity Zebra's washing day.
"One nice clean shirt," he counted.
"One spotless scarf. One—"

WHOOSH!

Suddenly a huge gust of wind blew all Zippity's clothes up in the air, towards the street.

"oh no!" yelled Zippity.

"Dear me," said Miss Cheetah.
"We'd better go after them."

Zippity and Miss Cheetah were racing
down the street when they spotted
Doctor Giraffe in his car.

"I've lost all my clothes!" wailed Zippity.
Then Doctor Giraffe pointed at the road.
"Look!" he said.

"It's my shirt!"
Zippity squealed happily.

Further down the road, Mister Elephant was reading his newspaper. **"Hey!"** called Zippity. "Have you seen any of my clothes?"

Mister Elephant peeled a sock off his paper. "I thought the news looked strange today," he chuckled. "I'd better come and help you."

As the four friends passed Professor Croc's house, they heard the sound of music.

"I've lost my clothes!" called Zippity.

"Have you seen any blowing past?"

"I wondered why the notes sounded odd," replied Professor Croc.
"This must be your tie!"

The five friends arrived
at the town hall.

What was
Mayor Monkey
laughing at?

"That's not a flag!"
giggled Zippity.

Mayor Monkey joined
the search party.

It wasn't long before they
spotted a scarf
in Lenny Lion's front garden...

...a jacket outside Papa Penguin's fish shop...

...and a hat at Madam Hippo's café.

"Thank you, everyone,"
grinned Zippity.

"I'm very lucky to have
such good friends."
Then everybody sat down for a well-deserved treat.

For Sebastian and Sophie
– CH

First published in 2009 by Scholastic Children's Books
Euston House, 24 Eversholt Street
London NW1 1DB
a division of Scholastic Ltd
www.scholastic.co.uk
London ~ New York ~ Toronto ~ Sydney ~ Auckland
Mexico City ~ New Delhi ~ Hong Kong

Text and illustrations copyright © 2009 Claire Henley

PB ISBN 978 1407 10665 6
HB ISBN 978 1407 10666 3

1 3 5 7 9 10 8 6 4 2

The moral rights of Claire Henley have been asserted.

Papers used by Scholastic Children's Books are made from wood grown in sustainable forests.